LEGO® CITY! It's a bustling town full of busy people with places to go and things to do. Some of those people have to go to the LEGO CITY bank to withdraw their money.

'I need to *withdraw* some money, too,' chuckled a crook disguised as a construction worker, who was sitting in a big bulldozer nearby.

Meanwhile, a crook disguised as an electrician nodded at a police officer before walking into the bank. The officer nodded back. He was keeping a close eye on everything.

'Hello, bank tellers!' said the electrician, waving to them as he strolled inside. The bank tellers all smiled and waved back.

'I'm here to . . . *fix* the security cameras!' he said, smirking to himself.

With the police officer outside, the electrician strolled down a hallway and found the security room. He slipped inside, closed the door and locked it. 'Well, that was easy!'

Inside, the electrician stared at the wall full of monitors. He could see everything going on inside the bank, and outside, too. Then he pulled out a really big wrench!

Smiling, the electrician said, 'Time to fix the security cameras . . .'

SMASH!

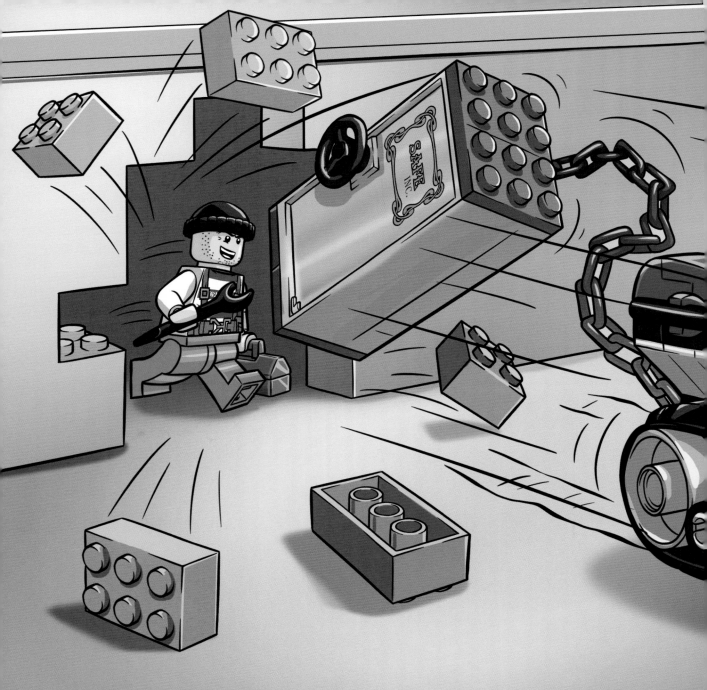

ZZZZZT! All the security cameras in the bank went dead!

Outside, the construction worker's mobile phone pinged with a message that said, 'Fixed!'

He quickly grabbed a heavy drill from the bulldozer and punched a big hole in the bank wall. He then fed a chain through the wall for the electrician to attach to the safe.

'Time for some *de*-construction!' the construction worker exclaimed. Then he drove the bulldozer forward and, a few seconds later, the safe smashed through the bank wall.

CRAAAASH!

The electrician ran through the hole in the wall to the bulldozer, where he joined the construction worker. They looked so much alike that they could have been twins!

'Open the safe, brother!' said the electrician.

'Will do right now, brother!' replied the construction worker.

Wait! They *were* twins!

The crooks opened the safe. They gasped when they looked inside . . .

The safe was empty!

'They tricked us!' grumbled the first crook.
'It's OK. I think I know where they've hidden the cash!' said the other crook, grinning. He pointed at a police truck, speeding away from the bank. The police were taking the money somewhere else!

'Stop! LEGO CITY police!' a police officer shouted.

The brothers started up the bulldozer and began to follow the police truck at a high speed.

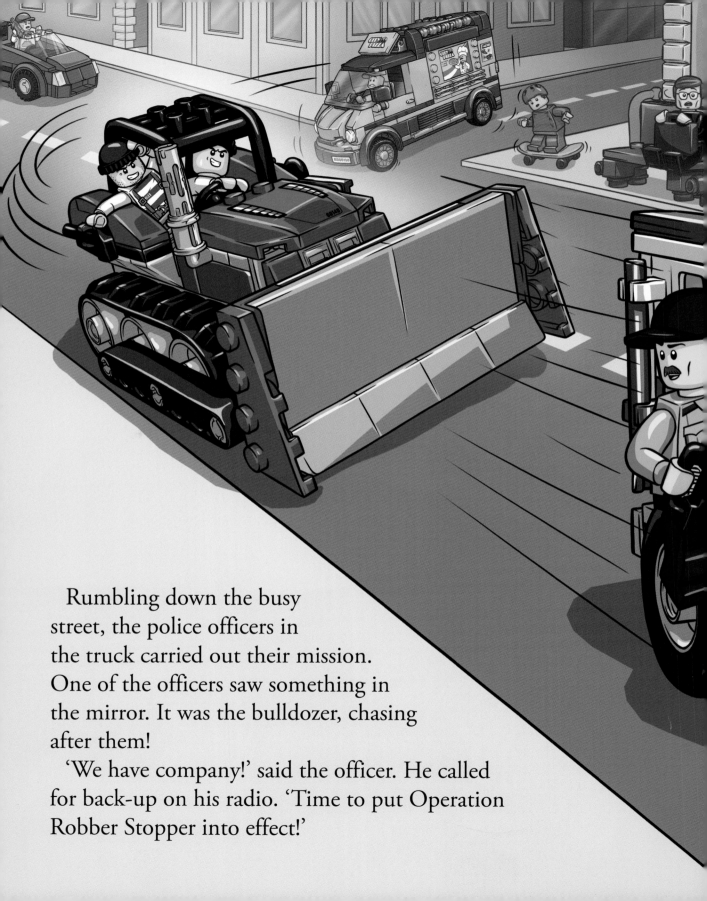

Rumbling down the busy
street, the police officers in
the truck carried out their mission.
One of the officers saw something in
the mirror. It was the bulldozer, chasing
after them!

'We have company!' said the officer. He called
for back-up on his radio. 'Time to put Operation
Robber Stopper into effect!'

The police truck rounded a corner and picked up speed. The bulldozer followed.

'That thing is more like a *race*dozer than a bulldozer,' said one police officer.

The crook who wasn't driving kept an eye out behind them for any trouble. He spied an identical police truck driving in the opposite direction! Even the licence plate was the same!

'That police truck has a twin!'
exclaimed the crook.
'Ah, you're just seeing things,'
replied his brother.

The police truck reached the outskirts of LEGO CITY, with
the bulldozer hot on its tail. The two vehicles zoomed down a long,
winding road.

'Let it roll!' the police officer in the truck called into his radio.
Suddenly, a big load of logs rolled in front of the bulldozer . . .
WHAM! The bulldozer rumbled over them.
CRASH! The bulldozer ploughed through a 'road closed' sign.
SMASH! A bunch of boulders rolled down a hill and rammed
into the bulldozer.

The police officers in the truck looked back at the bulldozer and chuckled.

'I think our roadblock was a *hit*,' said the first police officer.

The other officer laughed. 'They're going to love our next surprise.'

Meanwhile, the bad guys bulldozed along.

'Any minute now and that money will be ours!' said one of the crooks.

WHOP! WHOP! WHOP!
The sound of helicopter blades grew louder as a police helicopter hovered above the thieves. 'Attention, crooks!' a policewoman said over a loudspeaker. 'You are under arrest!'
One of the crooks turned round.

What did he see?

A horde of police were chasing them! Police cars, motorcycles, helicopters – you name it – were after the bad guys!

'We might be in trouble,' sighed the crook to his brother.

His brother revved the engine of the bulldozer. No way was he going to give up. He wanted that money! **VROOOOOM!**

The bulldozer closed in on the police truck. The money was within their reach! Suddenly, the bulldozer slid along the road, spinning in circles. What was going on?

It was the fire department! They were helping the police by spraying foam on to the road. The foam made the surface extremely slippery!

'We've got you now!' said the police officer in the helicopter.
She watched from high above as the bulldozer spun round and round,
and slid into an abandoned construction site.

The bulldozer landed on a wooden board leaning against a metal pipe,
which sent paint pots flying through the air.

One paint pot hit the controls of the cement mixer. Another turned the mixer on and sprayed cement all over the bulldozer!

The twins tried to bulldoze through but their 'racedozer' creaked to a halt as the cement hardened.

'We were so close!' groaned
the crook at the wheel.
'You were *never* close,' said a
police officer from the bank.
'The police truck you were
following was a decoy!'

'A *decoy*?' yelled the crook. 'You mean –'

'The truck we were driving was empty the whole time!' said the police officer. He opened the doors to show the twins. There was nothing inside! Other officers had used an identical truck to take the real safe that was full of money to a different bank.

'See? I told you the police truck had a twin!' the crook said to his brother, grumpily.

'You two will have a long time in prison to think about your crime,' said the officer. He put the crooks into the police trailer and locked the door.

'I'm done,' said one crook. 'No more robbing banks for me!'

'Why is that?' asked his brother.

'There's no money in it!' his twin replied, as the police trailer drove away.

THE END